Cat Alley

written and illustrated by **Ib Spang Olsen**
translated from the Danish by **Virginia Allen Jensen**

Coward, McCann & Geoghegan, Inc.   New York

First American Edition 1971
Illustrations and original Danish text copyright © 1968 by Ib Spang Olsen
First published in 1968 by Gyldendal, Copenhagen, Denmark
All rights reserved
Library of Congress Catalog Card Number: 73-161608
Printed in Denmark by Grafodan Offset, Vaerløse, Copenhagen

Martin and Laura and their father and mother moved into a new apartment building called High House. The first thing they did was look out of the windows.

"We're way up in the air," said Laura. "We can see everything from here."

"Yes, but there isn't much to look at," said Martin, "not in our yard. It's empty. But there's a cat!" He pointed to the old houses on the lot next door.

"Do you think we can find anyone to play with?" Laura asked.

"Let's go down and look," Martin said. "Maybe there's at least one child down there, so small we can't see him from here. We can take a closer look at the cat's house, too."

Martin and Laura stood in the middle of their yard and looked around.

"At least we have plenty of room," Laura said.

"And it's all boring," Martin answered. "I don't even feel like staying here."

"I suppose we can play with each other," Laura said. "We can sit in the sun and we can play ball and talk and things like that."

Martin didn't answer. So Laura turned to see what he was doing. Martin was gone!

"He's disappeared," she said to herself. "I'd better look for him."

So she left the yard.

From the street she could see the old buildings next door, with their slanting walls and drooping roofs, but she couldn't see Martin.

"It would be just like him to go into a shop like this one, full of strange things. He'd look at everything and try out all the chairs and couches, and not buy anything. He doesn't have a penny in his pocket. It's embarrassing to be the sister of a boy like that."

She went into the furniture shop.

Inside there were many old sofas and benches and cats. At the very back were a strange bed and a small fireman.

"Hey, this bed really works, just the way the pictures on the wall show it does. I got into these clothes fast."

"Oh," said Laura. "Is this your store?"

"No, and I'm not really a fireman. My name is Ida. This is the handyman's store, but we children from High House are the only ones who come here—and that new boy. He's coming back to try the bed."

"That must be my brother. I'm looking for him. So long!"

Laura waved good-bye to Ida and the cats.

Laura walked out of the store thinking,
"That was a funny place, with all those cats and the
fire-girl from High House. A bed like that would be handy
if you had to get up very early in the morning
and had trouble getting dressed.

"Maybe Martin went into the boot shop. He'd like shopping there, asking for things like seven-league boots, even though he can't buy them."

Laura opened the door and

stopped in surprise.

"How can you walk up there?" she asked the girl on the wall and the boy on the ceiling.

"I have borrowed some wall boots," said the girl. "It's fun to walk like a fly."

"And I borrowed ceiling boots," said the boy. "I like looking at things upside down."

"You may borrow some boots, too," said the lady. "Here is a pair of puddle boots. With them you can wade as deep as you want. The water will never go over the tops! Or you can borrow dancing boots or seven-league boots."

"Seven-league boots?" said Laura.

"Yes," said the lady, "but I haven't any of the seven-yard boots the new boy wanted. So he didn't stay long."

"He's just moved into High House," said the boy.

"That's probably my brother," Laura said. "I'm looking for him. I'd better go now, but I'd like to come back some other time."

She left the store filled with strange boots-to-borrow.

Back outside in the alley, Laura found more kittens and cats and boys and girls, but Martin wasn't there. She picked up a kitten and it seemed to like her.

"We're practicing the barrel organ," said two of the children. "Soon we'll be able to play 'Silent Night.'"

"We're polishing the handyman's car," said two other children. "Next year we'll see if it will run."

"My brother and I have just moved into High House," said Laura, "but my brother is missing right now."

"We're from High House, too," said the children. "That new boy who was here and tooted the horn must be your brother. He went to the backyard."

Laura hurried to the back of the house. "You're from High House, aren't you?" said the man coming up from the cellar. "I'm the handyman. There isn't any more room for me down in my workshop. It's full of children, but I did get this kangaroo stick greased."
"Come over here," the children shouted from the shed. "We're sharpening knives for mother and the Indians."

"We're finding old things in this chest," shouted some other children.
"I'm minding my own business," said the little boy looking out from behind the door.
"I'm looking for my brother Martin," said Laura.
"I saw him go into the workshop," said the boy with the hammer.
"My name is Eric.
I'll go down with you
if you like."
So Laura and Eric
went into the cellar.

It was dark down there, but Laura could see some children building something big. It looked like a machine.

"What is that?" Laura asked the boy on the ladder. "Is it yours?"

"It's our Adalusian Lens Press," he answered. "Can't you see that?"

"No, this is the first time I have ever seen an Abalensian Loose Presher. What's it for?"

"We'll find out when we finish it. But who are you? We can't let everybody see our invention."

"I'm Laura and I'm looking for my brother Martin."

"Oh, him," said the boy. "Yeah, we greased the buzzer gears and the rotaters with him."

Laura was frightened, but the boy inside the firebox said, "Don't worry; Victor is always teasing. Your brother went up to see the Skipper."

"Thanks for telling me," said Laura. "I think that's a good Aloosy-crusher. I'll come back to see it work."

She and Eric went outside.

"There's the Skipper," said Eric. "In the old days he was a pirate. He has a wooden leg because a shark ate the real one."

"Ahoy, Eric! Come on up, miss!" the Skipper shouted.

"Do we dare go up there?" Laura whispered.

"The steps are safe," Eric answered.

"Welcome aboard, folks!" the Skipper shouted. "Set your course straight ahead!"

Laura and Eric went inside.
"This is just like the cabin of a real ship," Laura thought. She was almost sure that she felt the floor rocking.

They asked about Martin.

"Try looking up on deck," the Skipper said. "It's blowing up from the northeast."

Eric and Laura pulled themselves up the steps to the deck.

Laura stopped in the hatchway, astonished.

"Where are we?" She steadied herself.

"This is the Skipper's old ship. He sailed it for so many years that he couldn't bear to part with it. Now he lets us kids from High House sail it."

"Pirates to the leeward!" shouted a boy.

"Shall I call the Skipper?" Laura asked.

"He's not coming. He's afraid of getting seasick."

"I want to go back.
I have to find my brother."
"Your brother went down the hatch
up front," said a girl. "You can go the same way."

So they did.

Laura landed at the foot of the Skipper's steps, with a kitten in her arms and without Eric.

"How strange," she thought. "But I like cats. And Martin likes horses. He is sure to be in one of those stables."

She asked the cowboys if they had seen a boy in a hurry, one who always disappeared just when you were about to catch up with him.

"Yeah," said the cowboys. "Go right through the swinging door."

Laura went into the nearest shed. It was small and dark inside, and the door on the other side of the room hung askew. She opened it cautiously . . .

and found herself standing on a prairie! The tall grass rustled in the wind, and she held onto her hair, while cowboys and horses whirled around her with lassos and guns.

"Have you seen a boy without a horse?" Laura shouted to a sheriff who was riding past.

"Yep, but he found a horse and jumped right into the saddle. He went thataway," the sheriff said, pointing his thumb toward a log cabin.

Laura trudged across the prairie and went into the cabin. It was empty, so she opened another door and

stepped out into a garden. Everywhere Laura looked she saw more and more cats, and more and more children from High House. They were all friendly, and a boy offered her some fried bananas.
"Oh, look," said Laura. "The sun is shining in your tree!"
"Ummm," said a girl. "We hung it there ourselves. You may climb the tree if you like, but I have this chair for the whole day."
"Why do you have an alarm clock in the middle of the garden?" Laura asked.

"It rings every sixty minutes and the handyman comes up to call out the hour. That's how we know when it's time to go home," said a boy, poking his head out of the ground.
"Have you seen my brother Martin?" Laura asked him.
"Yes, he was down here in our dugout, but I think he's gone home now. He had lost his sister."

Laura went back to High House and up to their apartment, and Martin was there.

They had supper with their mother and father, and just before they went to bed, they looked out the windows again. There wasn't much to see, just the old houses with their slanting walls and drooping roofs. And two cats.

Martin grinned. "Plenty of kids to play with," he said.

"And animals," Laura agreed. "And lots of things we don't know about yet."

They closed the windows, and that night they dreamed about tomorrow

in CAT ALLEY.

About the Author

IB SPANG OLSEN's talents are many and varied. In addition to the numerous juvenile and adult books he has illustrated, including twelve authored by himself, he has done several murals, designed many posters and ceramic pieces, executed independent lithographs, and developed his own technique for mass production of quality graphic art.

Recognized as a leading Danish graphic artist, Ib Spang Olsen has accumulated many prizes and awards: He is a two-time runner up for the Hans Christian Andersen medal, and five of his books were chosen best children's picture book of the year by the Danish Ministry of Culture.